EDEN 12

By

Paul Cooke

Chapter 1

They came out of the ground like rats out of a sinking ship. Deep underground they start their journey then fly out into the light. It is always light a soft glow that doesn't alter, an orange, blue haze that hangs over the planet like a soft night light, no creature has seen the night sky for many years. The cars continue to stream out of the wormhole with lights blazing. Once on the surface they quickly join each other to form a never ending train of car pods that shoot across the horizon at break neck speeds. The advent of nuclear fusion chips gave the humans their power source that runs everything now, the only drawback being that the planet is so contaminated it does literally glow from nuclear waste products…The planet and its inhabitants over hundreds of years have come to adapt and subterranean lifestyles exist many miles below the surface away from the pollution. Here you can remove your surface suit with its nuclear powered filtration system and walk free and breath the cool, cool air of the earth….Some explorers have even gone to depths of thousands of miles under ground and discovered vast caves and lakes with some sustaining life forms. We only travel on the surface now as it is quicker than the tunnels frequently jammed with slow moving traffic and prone to disruption from water and other elements…

The car pods now can more or less travel on anything as they have a gravity down force control as part of their design that makes the car pod act like a limpet on any surface…These vehicles have their limitations though and given that you are not on a relatively flat surface they will lose their grip with devastating consequences as they can reach speeds of over 1000 kilometers per hour. Some people have tried to navigate the seas and mountains with the vehicles and as soon as you encounter choppy seas or rugged terrain then the pod will just launch itself into the air at 45 degrees and literally take off, give that there is no standard flying mechanism then you are at the mercy of gravity…The military pods are designed to fly but these are only issued to the armed forces as it is perceived that it would be too dangerous to offer these models to the general public…The car pods link by radar and once out of the ground hook up to each other until you disengage the tracking system and steer out of the pod train at your destination, this is automatically done as soon as you indicate your intention to exit, you then hook up to further car pod trains until docked at your destination. Given that the atmosphere is so bad other than the military pods no flying is allowed and in some respects was superseded by the nuclear powered vehicles that can reach far greater speeds then any plane used to, in fact the standard issue car pod reaches speeds equal to the former fighter aircraft long ago and military flying pods often reach mach two and their during their missions.

The planet now as seen from satellites orbiting earth is peppered with millions of worm holes as if the earth has become a huge pin cushion, each wormhole services the entire population of the world that lives its life mainly underground, we started to shift our resources underground many years ago due to the contamination that we could no longer control. It is now possible to circumnavigate the globe via tunnel such is the extent of the underground networks. Along with the visible holes vast surface plants emit streams of waste gasses that sparkle and fizz as the chemicals react with the planets polluted atmosphere. Not many creatures can live on the surface of the planet but some have transmutated to survive brief excursions and most sea life that wasn't killed has managed to create new life in the thick polluted grime that we used to know as the sea..

Eden 12 wakes up searches for the tube attached to his bio port this has been feeding him all the daily nutrients no one sits down and eats meals anymore…He also removes the other two tubes from his genitals and anus that have been collecting his waste products during his sleep…he sits up and for a while scans the room, gets up slowly and walks over to his clothes hung up across the other side of the room. His suit reacts to his presence and can starts to read his vital signs. He pulls the suit over his skin and the suit goes to work monitoring his body, it instantly makes a connection to the ram pool and Eden's movements will be tracked until he takes of the suit. It is illegal to remove the suits and anyone caught without a suit on outside of their accommodation faces prosecution and loss of privileges…Eden checks his weapon and radar data and starts to read his mission brief…he has to rendezvous at 0900 with his unit 3 clicks away and await further instructions. Eden is a warrior class citizen and has been genetically constructed for the role. His names numeric value is an indication of this and he makes up a unit of Eden's all allocated a separate number and sometimes a letter to denote their rank in Eden's case he is basic warrior class material. The red dot in the corner of his space is alerted to his movements and it has sent a report to the commander of the unit that Eden has woken up and has also relayed the fact that he has read his mission statement. This maneuver today is somewhat of a covert action as today is a public holiday to mark the birthday of the founders of DNA mapping, 'James Watson and Francis Crick'. On this day most of the public will be underground leaving the surface free for the military to pursue their objectives easier…Eden's only domestic task is to clean his bio tube and waste tubes with an antibacterial agent that he sprays on and leaves to get to work, the liquid has hundreds of nano bots that have been held in a stasis until the solution is applied, once sprayed into the atmosphere they quickly get to work hunting down and bacteria and eliminating it with a deadly chemical that they continually reproduce until the task is complete….Eden grabs his (Environmental Mapping Device) and opens the door to his space and walks across a brightly lit hall to his car pod…The pod recognizes his presence just like his suit and prepares the vehicle for its journey the pod picked up the information from the mission brief sent to Eden and is ready to deliver him to his objective…Eden plugs his EMD into the dashboard and braces himself for takeoff, the audio bleeps signal the pods readiness as the four tones increase in pitch and volume warning him of departure, at the final tone a high pitched and barely audible sound his pod blasts out of the wormhole and up towards the phosperous glow of the planets sky…as the pod bounces over the edge of the hole Eden momentarily glances an object to his left a mutated animal still roaming the planet's surface, many years ago a lot of people refused to go underground and form the new world and the remnants of their actions still remain with mutated pets and other domestic creatures roaming around adapting and surviving in an environment that was thought to be un survivable for any living creature, needless to say all the human beings on the planet failed to survive more than 100 years or more with no trace of any of their ancestors from this period…The creature fails to get out of the way of the pod in time and splatters across the windscreen as the pod reaches mach 2 the last remaining smear recedes quickly and its gone…Eden curses, 'I hate it when that happens' he shouts out loud'…and punches the button to activate his EMD. The EMD starts to feed his coordinates into the RAM pool a vast data storage that doesn't ever sleep, and has been active for thousands of years now. Eden's ancestor started mapping the sea bed with EMD's and that data was auto sent back to a database that eventually transmuted thousands of years later into the RAM pool….The EMD still continues its work and wherever any military pod goes then the EMD's sensors relay back all the information to the RAM pool and it is stored and updated as appropriate. The entire surface of the planet has been scanned this way and 99.9% of the surface including ocean floors has been recorded and noted giving Eden's commanders instant information both visual and statistical on any square inch of the planet's surface…The EMD responds back to his punch, please activate the system prior to leaving base…Eden know his commander will have picked this up and responds, 'disturbance and encounter with life-force on exit caused the delay'…The red eye in his pod blinks and Eden knows his words have been recorded and his commander will pick them up…Mach 3 and the pod launches off the ground and folds its wings gracefully out and races to his rendezvous point…Eden's sensors pick up the members of his unit a hundred strong pods all converging on at the destination, the pod brakes sharply makes contact with the surface again, pulls in its wings and shoots into a wormhole, the pod races into a parking bay at 5the bottom of the hole and Eden steps out surrounded by fellow members of his unit who greet each other as they stream into the HQ for their briefing.....Eden's one hundred strong unit assemble in under a circular dome and they are greeted by their commander Eden 1. The ranking system as with all the designs of the inhabitants of the new world order are simplistic, a simple one embedded on the suit of the commanding officer is all that is needed to convey his authority, every other warrior is subordinated accordingly from two onwards. Given that Eden 1 is killed in action then Eden 2 assumes command, genetically the warriors have been bred this way as the higher the number more leadership skills have been bred into them to carry out the associated tasks, hence the current 'in' jokes about Eden 100's being the grunts of the fighting units. The characteristics of the later Eden numbers do vary with them assuming more of a stocky and aggressive feature than the earlier numbered warriors. Eden 1 emits a shrill call from deep within and the unit falls silent, the unit leader speaks. 'We are today going above the clouds'; the unit audibly gasps in unison. 'We have been designated coordinates of an area that has seen recent activity with creatures that have been attacking our worker units high up in the mountain ranges mapping these sectors, your pods have been programmed with all the mission data and I want an immediate rendezvous in this area as soon as possible, please check out weapons on your way out as I expect encounters with hostile entities, dismissed. The whole unit swarms back out of the dome and as they file past the doors out to their craft a tube is dispensed into their hand, they each check the information on a panel to see that the charge is up and make sure the safety is set to 'on'. This nuclear tube launcher is capable if set to 'high' can destroy an armored tank at 100 yards so the weapon is treated with the up most respect. In the pod cars the warriors carry a further four launchers embedded into the four sides of their craft however these are of a more substantial design and capability than the hand held launchers and can nuke an entire colony in seconds given the need. Eden 12 jumps into his pod, places the tube launcher in his suit, and hits his start button. The pod's guidance system feeds back the coordinates to him as 100 pod cars simultaneously eject from the wormhole and head for the sky. Once out of the hole the pods form a complete and perfect circle and race across the ground until take off is achieved, they level out at two thousand feet and the warriors relax into the mission…The warrior units can be scrambled at short notice if needed and are so designed for the mission briefing to be relayed by Eden 1 on the fly, given that each member resides within 1 mile of each other, then a warrior circle pack can rendezvous in minutes to ward off any attack…The unit approaches its destination and breaks through the cloud cover, settling just a few meters from the clouds surface gliding in and out of white puffs of cloud vapor in an attempt to remain as less a visible target as possible. On the horizon Eden 12 spots a mountain peak topped with snow coming into view, as they approach the size of the mountain range becomes apparent with a vast backbone of the mountain extended for hundreds of miles at above the cloud level….As the audio alarms signal that the coordinates have been reached Eden 1 shouts his order to, 'be vigilant men'. The circle pack quickly disperses and the pods go into defense positions along the ridge, slowly descending until the pods gravity pull kicks in and sucks them to the mountain like limpets…Eden 1 barks another order, 'Eden 12 to 35 engage with the environment and ascend the peak to provide an observation post command'. Eden 12 jumps out of his pod and as he hits the ground his boots equipped with the same suction technology activate and allow him to run up the sheer snow and ice face towards the summit of the mountain. As he gets higher and as he feels his energy decrease a hood auto detracts from the back of his suit and encases his head feeding much needed oxygen and warmth to his suit. His boots are so designed to vary the input needed and auto adjust so that the minimum of effort is required for the suction to take effect, but he is finding it hard work today as the conditions are so extreme and he is having to put an enormous effort into his accent, as they all simultaneously reach the summit, they assume defense 360 degree positions and activate their binocular lenses fitted to their eyelids, essentially a second clear eyelid with a binocular function embedded into it. A further third eyelid was also genetically created based around animal designs that give protection in combat situations. Eden 12 and his team scan the lower depths of the mountain range…as they get their bearings the terrain comes into view and they start to make out the fauna and flora in a green lush valley, as the beauty of the scenery takes them by surprise for a brief moment, a loud scream is heard and a gush of wind alerts Eden 12 to an object flying in from his left, he instinctively dives down as an eagle swoops over his head and floats along the mountain range gliding along and making good use of the air currents, it suddenly dives and heads for the valley floor….Eden 12 reports in, 'nothing to report sir, just some huge creature just buzzed us and has descended to the valley below'…Eden 1 responds, 'Roger that Eden 12' remain vigilant'….

Chapter 2

As the team squat on the top of the mountain attached precariously it seems to the frozen summit a small figure in orange robes walks briskly along the valley floor stepping calmly and efficiently moving flora and fauna out of his way with the end of a long staff in ever moving circles. Eden 12 is the first to spot the movement and calls it in, 'Eden 1, Eden 12 reporting life signs on the valley floor at EMD reading 324,233 awaiting orders, over. 'Eden 12, intercept the life form and capture alive, I repeat capture alive'…Eden 12 is the best close combat exponent in the team and he has the highest chance of capturing the life form given his DNA. Certain warrior castes such as Eden 12 have ingenious mod's such as Kevlar strength membranes designed to seal their vital organs and cavities so that any strikes by knifes, spears or other sharp objects fail to penetrate and damage their internal organs. In times of close combat Eden 12's testicles retract automatically and a Kevlar strength membrane covers the hole left by the retraction. Further to the additional scoping membrane in his eyes another such protective shield covers the eyes when in combat. Every other part of Eden 12's body, wherever there is a cavity or vulnerable part such as his throat is covered by this protective membrane that will even deflect bullets at a distance. The skull of these warrior classes are also covered entirely with the same material hence the jokes amongst other classes about not worrying about dropping Eden's on their heads when they are ejected from the birthing tanks…In fact most Eden's are literally thrown out of the tanks such is their known resilience to any damage physical damage…

Eden 12 detaches his nuclear suction system and is at the valley floor in seconds, as the craft sucks itself into the soft damp mud of the valley floor, Eden 12 hits his ejection strap and is catapulted out of his pod in a 360 degree arc that makes its way behind the life form and lands Eden 12 a few meters away from the target. Eden is surprised at the life forms appearance as it is human and he hesitates for just one second as he takes in similar features to his own. A perfectly round face with no hair just a shiny head, no expression and no element of surprise or shock on the face, Eden 12 looks down on his subject who is at least one meter shorter. Eden 12 doesn't see the wooden staff arrive in the next second as it penetrates his helmet shield and is aimed just to the left of his chin and in the only soft fleshy non protected area of his body. He doesn't get to experience any further sensation as the wooden staff delivers enough energy into this point to upset the blood balance between his skull and the rest of his body and he passes out instantly with the blow…In the third second of the encounter his assailant has swung his robes around Eden 12 and they both disappear into a small hole in the ground a few steps away….

Eden 12 slowly awakes and his suit has been removed he is lying on a small cotton bed roll in a huge cavern reverberating to the chanting of hundreds of creatures all dressed in the same orange robes…As he sits up he notices wafts of smoke streaming up and into a small vent hole in the ceiling and his senses pick up the sweet pungent aroma…He cannot see any visible way out of the area and given that one of these creatures managed to knock him unconscious so quickly he was hardly in a position to escape given hundreds of them are sitting yards away from him. A loud bell pierces the ambience and they stop there chant and start to move off their cotton mats and file out of the area without giving him much notice to him…He recognizes his assailant who approaches him and bows his head as he approaches, from deep within his billowing sleeve he reveals a bowl that seems to contain dead parts of plants that have a strange smell and consistency. The creature takes the contents of the bowl and gestures to him, adding some of the bowls contents to his lips and placing it in his mouth. Eden 12 stands back in horror as the creature moves his mouth and the contents of his mouth disappear. The creature places the bowl on the floor bows again and leaves him. Eden 12 looks at the bowl for a long time and as nothing seems to be moving inside he grabs it and pokes the different colored textures, puts some of the substance to his nose and smells it…The smell is nothing like he has ever encountered yet he feels somehow drawn to the smell and copies the creature placing a small amount in his mouth. He feels his mouth fill with fluid and he is compelled to move his mouth and starts to chew the food, Eden 12 swallows his mouthful and is instantly sick ejecting the contents of his mouth across the room…

Eden 12 is stirred from his sleep by the rushing of feet in the dark, he has some night vision capabilities and tracks the creatures moving around the space, clouds of smoke billow out from certain areas and a spark of light erupts from one corner as flames around the room light up his surroundings. Eden 12 this time stands up and as he does so he is aware that he to has been dressed in a similar orange robe tied in the middle with a course piece of band…Again he recognizes his assailant and he approaches again in the same manner bowing his head and as if by magic circles a cup of liquid in front of him and offers it to him with his head bowed…Eden 12 takes the cup and places it to his lips and drinks the liquid, it burns the back of his throat as it goes down and warms his stomach area and he feels somewhat better after drinking it. The creature gestures to him to sit by pointing to his mat and pointing to his fellow creatures all now sitting crossed legged on the floor….Eden 12 adopts the same position and a bell strike pierces the room and there is silence until the creatures start chanting. Eden 12 is silent and observes….The final bell tolls and the creatures again file out in silence his assailant approaches and after bowing gesticulates for him to follow him…He picks up two wooden staffs as he leaves the room and Eden 12 becomes fearful of these sticks as he follows at some distance behind him…They navigate a series of dark dank and dimly lit caves and tunnels finally arriving at the foot of some steep and narrow steps that seem to stretch to the heavens…His assailant seems to float up the steps as he finds it hard to keep pace. As they near the last top step the creature penetrates the roof with his two staffs and fly's out into bright sunlight and lands a few meters from the entrance. Eden 12 squints until his protective membrane in his eye cancels out the bright light and he stands shakily staring at his surroundings….is his life to end here he thinks?

The creature throws him one of the wooden staffs and Eden 12 catches it feeling the smooth and cool surface as it slides through his grip until he grips tighter and it stops its movement. He briefly catches the creatures staff as it glances of his skull and he instinctively reacts with a squat and a roll but as he regains all sense of his balance and composure his adversary is behind him and he feels another blow directly across his back that sends him forward and into a flying position….As Eden 12 flies across the lush green vegetation he sees a huge bird flying and dipping into the valley below…He expects this to be his final vision with his execution very imminent as he cannot even begin to track or stop his attacker as he seems to be moving and operating in a different time and place and even before Eden 12 can react he has moved like some smirking time traveler ready to strike him again…Eden 12 just lands and stays there expecting to be killed with the next blow…but all he hears is a creature piercing the air with its cries and he gets to his feet looks around and his attacker has gone…Eden 12 starts to take in his surroundings and notices that to his left are more steps that seem to lead up the mountain, he activates his membrane to scope further and beyond his immediate mountain top he spies a snow covered peak with what looks like his teams pod marks still imprinted in the snow, if only he can get to his pod now, he runs upwards to get a better vantage point….

As he reaches the summit of this mountain he reaches a plateau and there are a series of rocks, large rectangular in shape smooth and white in appearance shimmering in the sunlight. As he looks over the edge he sees the creature below with its wide wings extended circling around making screeching noises as it fly's further up towards him….It flies and swoops very close to him and then ascends on thermal drafts upwards and across to the mountain opposite…He activates his scoping membrane follows the line of the mountain down and sees the exact spot where he was attacked, and there is his pod. Somehow there is a connection between the two mountains that he needs to find, to escape…Eden 12 without his suit and technology cannot traverse the mountains and he is left to ponder how he can get up to his craft to signal to his team that he has survived the mission….As he looks around the edge of the summit he notices a series of steps that literally circle the mountain, he has found his way down. Eden 12 finds the top of the steps and hurls himself down the steps, sometimes body surfing the smooth marble white steps and landing with a crunch directly into a lower wall…As he reaches the bottom of the last step he lands hard after sliding down the last series of steps into soft material that forms a crater as he lands and billows up fine hard particles that bounce of his protective eye membrane as he falls head long into the ground…….As he shakes of the particles he spots a creature dressed in white robes flowing around his body as he moves backwards and forwards across a fine surface that borders a lake that mirrors and reflects the vastness of the mountains behind him….. The creature dressed in white has a shiny stick like weapon that glints and reflects the bright light around him…

The creature approaches him and Eden 12 starts to get ready for his execution as to him this weapon if more advanced than the wooden stick is bound to be the weapon that finally kills him…He adopts a fighting stance to at least defend himself prior to his execution. Eden 12 does not see the sword circle his arm or the creature get into position and finds the tip of the sword pressing gently at the same point that the creature struck him when he intercepted it. He waited for the weapon to penetrate and kill him, but he feels the tip recede and the weapon disappear behind the creature and into his robes…The creature bows low and waves his hand for him to follow, as he follows him around the bay he notices a round shaped craft bouncing up and down on the water…The creature steps into the water and holds the craft stopping its movement….with a nod of his head the creature motions for Eden 12 to get in, Eden 12 complies with his wishes. Eden 12 sits in the small craft and is handed another wooden staff with a flat bottom surface. The creature points with his sword to a tree standing with its branches bowed and hanging dripping into the water, and motions for him to use his wooden paddle…Eden 12 sinks his paddle into the water and applies some pressure and finds that his small craft moves towards his objective, he paddles harder and heads towards the tree…The willow tree billows into the water and its branches trail and swirl around the water in the mountain breeze as Eden 12 precariously climbs out of his craft and sets of at a blistering pace towards his pod. It is good to feel his feet on the hard earth and he feels once again in control and strong he uses all of his recently stored energy to make quick progress smashing branches and obstacles out of his way like a charging rhino..

As he approaches the pod with his orange robes streaming behind him he notices that the machine does not recognize him without his suit and he finds the marks for his fingers on the cockpit, once lined up the biometric recognition subsystem actives the pods nuclear energy cell and the cockpit opens and the pods starts its reactor..Eden 12 jumps into the pod in one leap and settles into the pod as he engages thrust and searches for a short runway to take off, his communication light flickers; he has been picked up by his commander. Eden 12 settles for the route he came through and picks his way through the forest back to the lake, on the shoreline he guns the pod across the water and achieves lift and takes off heading vertically towards the cloud cover. As he is thrust back into his seat his commander's image appears on the pod dashboard and he asks Eden 12 to report in. 'Sir, I have managed to escape from my captors and my suggested ETA back at HQ is 20 clicks. Unfortunately my suit was taken and most of my functionality has been removed, can I request a replacement on arrival please sir?'..His commander smiles and welcomes Eden 12 back, 'Eden 12 report to the debriefing room as soon as you engage your pod at HQ and I will arranged for a replacement suit to be sent there for you, well done Eden 12...'Thank you sir' Eden 12 stares at the panel as his commanders face disappears going over and over his experiences in the cave ready for his de-briefing, trying to remember every strange details of his capture.

He looks down at his orange robes and the tears and rips all over the cloth from the race through the forest. The material still emits a smell of the incense that the creatures burned, this helps him recall other moments as he was drifting out of consciousness and he sinks into a deep contemplation. His pod signals that he is in range of HQ and starts to auto descend. As he breaks the cloud cover he is struck by the grey and black surface of the planet with its tangible phosphorescent hue that circles the globe in stark contrast to the world he has just returned from with its lush green vegetation and ice clean mountain lake...He observed the entry point into the HQ and takes over manual control as the pod speeds into the ground and he docks the craft. As he gets out of the pod, workers stare at the sight of his orange colored robes as he briskly walks down the runway towards the de-briefing room. He finds a strange uniqueness about his presence in the HQ as if he is a ghost, no security has picked him up due to not having his suit on as he notices the red security lights remaining static, and they have not detected him. As he enters the room his commander and Eden 2, 3 & 4 are sat around the huge circle space that is used for strategy meetings. Eden 1 notes his attire and asks him to sit down and quickly bring them up to speed on the enemy position. As Eden 12 replies the circle space is brought to life with the visual of Eden 12 as he descended towards the valley floor. 'Sir I was captured and over whelmed by a superior enemy who utilized or carried no weaponry or with any visible defense mechanisms other than sticks'. Eden 12 continues without a pause. 'However Sir I was unharmed from the very start and only knocked unconscious by my attacker, when I came to, I was looked after very well and no use of torture prevailed'. Eden 1 looks quizzically at him, 'you are saying Eden 12 that the enemy whilst superior to any fighter we have they did not do you no harm and let you go?' 'Sir when I was taken from deep within the mountain back into the forest I was again challenged by the same monk that captured me, and I was expecting this to be my execution as there was absolutely no way I could defend myself or inflict any harm on this monk?' Eden 12 did the fighters have any visible means off leaving their location? 'No sirs they are entirely sustained by their environment above the clouds and it seemed like they do not go any further than the cloud cover'. As the commanders review the last footage of Eden 12 being knocked unconscious by his attacker and analyze the way that Eden 12 is dragged into a small hole in the forest floor, Eden 1 points to his suit hung up in the corner of the room, 'Your suit Eden 12, please put it on straight away and report to the medical lab for analysis. 'Thank you sir', Eden 12 grabs his suit and makes his way towards the lab.

As Eden 12 walks into the lab and heads for a changing cubicle he spies the red lights flicker as they start to track his suit. As soon as he puts on his suit it goes to work monitoring his vital functions and the information has been passed to a technician before he has even climbed onto the monitoring table. The table itself is suspended in mid air via gravity fields and can be used for 360 degree operations by equipment that hovers and circles around the body; all activated by technicians who merely monitor the equipment as all the decisions are guided by the operating systems computer. As he lies there suspended the robots around him inject nano bots into his body tissue and they quickly go to work repairing his damaged muscle and skin cells. His overall health and organ functionality is checked and any deficiency is repatriated via the connecting tubes to his body that re-supplies essential nutrients for his body to function at its maximum capacity. As Eden 12 lies on the table he thinks of the people he left behind and how different their world was to his, yet they had a superiority that he couldn't quite fathom?

Chapter 3

Eden 12 sits in his home container holding the robes he managed to hang onto, he hooks them onto a frame on the wall and they hang there as testimony to his experience, he didn't dream it. Eden 12 activates his viewing circle and it glows white waiting for his input. Eden 12 starts issuing commands to the system, 'Tribes, warriors, religion, ancients….the viewing circle flickers and then zooms in on some text, Taoist warrior monks BC 4000….'Play' Footage of martial artists appear dressed in similar robes as he had hung up, they spin, jump and run with a variety of weapons and he notices the wooden staff used by his attacker, 'Freeze'. Eden 12 poured over the image, it was an exact likeness to the monk he had met, ancient humans living thousands of years ago but incredible fighters. But what about the chanting he thought, was this a link to their prowess? 'Chanting, group talking, speaking together', the viewing circle talked back to Eden 12, 'this is a form of group exercise that ancient human tribes used to practice, this was called praying, also known as mantra….It was a form of what was called a religion that different human beings practiced and had a general outlook attached to it that was perceived as a so called spiritual practice or else a worship of some text or deity…'Eden 12 somewhat confused asks more questions, 'Deity; what's is a deity, the viewing circle blinks, and responds. "A deity was something that ancient humans connected to and collectively worshiped by chanting mantras, or by praying. 'Show' Eden 12 excitedly barks, the viewing circle plays a scene of monks dressed in orange robes sitting crossed legged chanting mantras accompanied by other monks banging an instrument in time with the chant. Transfixed Eden 12 watches, then a piercing bell cuts through the air, he laughs. That was it he had discovered a lost settlement of monks that had survived thousands of years away from earth and all its upheavals…'Eden 12 remained curious, 'Show me chanting text, 'unavailable' the system responded, 'Show me prayer text' Eden 12 repeated, 'Unavailable' the machine responded. Eden 12 sat back briefly and shouted. 'Play Chanting, Play Mantras'…The system played back the scene of monks in their temple chanting….'Save chanting to RAM as Chant 1, Eden 12'. Your file is stored into RAM as Chant 1, Eden 12. 'Repeat Chant 1'

Eden 12 listened and started mouthing the chant copying the monks…Seta – Ma Ka – Han, NYA-HA-RA-MI,-TA, Shin, GYO….'Pause Chant 1', Eden 12 repeated the chant out loud….'Seta – Ma KA – Han, NYA-HA-RA-MI,-TA, Shin, GYO'….Eden 12 for effect gets up and puts on the robes and sits down crossing his legs on the floor and repeats the first part of the mantra, 'Seta – Ma KA – Han, NYA-HA-RA-MI,-TA, Shin, GYO'….Eden 12 smiles at the sounds coming from his mouth and laughs out loud at his discovery….

Eden 12 gets up and takes of his threadbare orange robe and throws it onto his bed and walks out of his container and into the cool of the underground cave he inhabits. He heads for a clear plastic type tube that is built into the cave wall and opens a catch that allows him to sit on a transparent seat that is itself inside a transparent egg shaped pod. He keys into the pad on the side of the egg pod his reference 334,456 and the egg pod shoots downwards searching for his destination. At breakneck speed it converges with other similar pods and Eden 12 smiles at the different people he bumps into as the egg pod changes direction, stops at a junction, then throws him back downwards into a dive and then it suddenly brakes sharply an stops in a gliding hydraulic motion that he always finds reassuring. Eden 12 pushes the door of the egg pod and walks into the bright sunlight of the recreation arena, with its huge ultra violet spheres injecting sunlight into the area twenty four seven. He walks along the exercise route that skirts the beach area and makes his way onto the bright white sand and feels his body weight shift as he tries to maintain his balance, he loves to walk on the sand and he enjoys the shifting feeling it gives him as he tries to maintain his speed. Most of the people on the beach scatter as he approaches and give him a wide berth as they can never tell if he is working, an occupational hazard of a warrior clone. He walks along and loves watching the beautiful white and olive skinned females lying naked on the rocks with their perfect breasts and buttocks on display as the males try and get their attention by showing off the latest in muscular implants that they have invested in. The only downside to it all is that they are all perfectly formed and the DNA specifications have been so finely tuned that there is not much to distinguish each male or female from another. Some of the population has old genetic DNA modifications built in at birth as a request from a parent that wants to influence the generation and you can tell these parental experiments exist and in some respects it has caused somewhat of an underclass with the child going through incredible taunting and teasing as they grow up. The majority of the populations stick to the near perfect formula just to satisfy their own requirements and in some respects their own peace of mind knowing that they are one hundred percent perfect in every way…

Eden 12 wades into the water as the wave's crash against him; he pushes and punches his way through the waves loving the resistance the water gives him. His protective shields auto activate with the activity and he kicks into the soft sand and dives through the waves into the water making his way at an alarming rate towards the sea floor. Eden 12 has another slight modification on his hands and feet, tiny webbing that allows him to powerfully grab handfuls of water and glide effortlessly along, he is also equipped with a gill just behind each ear and this allows him to filter the water and stay on the sea bed a lot longer than his cousins. Eden 12 catches up with a shoal of fish and dives straight through them feeling the fish bounce and dart of his face, he then heads straight up towards the sunlight and punches through the water head first rising twenty to thirty feet into the air and landing with a controlled impact with hardly a ripple slicing back into the water. Eden 12 heads back to shore and surfs the sea bed crashing his body against the sand and rocks as he goes and without stopping shoots out of the water scattering people left right and centre as he buries into the sand. Eden 12 loves swimming and shakes off the sand like a dog scattering people again as they get covered with a fine sand dusting. Eden 12 smiling, walks again pacing through the sand and finally back onto the harder surfaces and heads back to the egg pods built into the cave walls…Eden 12 still with a beaming smile on his face, punches in his coordinates and heads back home.

Eden 12 sits in front of his viewing circle and studies more film footage of the ancient civilizations he has discovered and as he watches some monk fly along the ground and sweep his opponent onto his back, Eden 1 breaks the picture and appears. 'Eden 12 can you please report to HQ in the next twenty clicks, your orders will be presented at the briefing. 'Yes Sir, Leaving right away'. Eden 1 smiles 'Eden 12, bring along the orange robes you picked up on the last mission'. Eden 12 grabs the robes and flies out of the door into his pod and blasts out of the ground and without skirting the road track gets airborne and into the highest speed his machine can achieve. As he backs the power off Eden 12 notices that no other warriors are present or making their way to the briefing and as he shoots back into the ground and docks with the HQ. Eden 12 jumps out of his craft and makes his way along the corridor to the briefing room. Eden 1, 2, 3, and 4 are sat in a room waiting for him. 'Sit down

Eden 12; we have a special assignment for you'. Eden 12 sits in anticipation. 'Eden 12 you are to proceed to these coordinates just south of the mountain area that we engaged with on the last mission'. 'The destination is a river that winds its way through the mountains and into the lake that you mentioned in your report'. 'From here you will make contact with the ancient civilization and report back after thirty days at the same coordinates that you started from'. 'It is imperative that you learn as much as you can about this civilization and report back with as much information as you can get about the species'. 'Given that they are a superior warrior class and have so far been actively engaged in peaceful existence above the clouds then we will not be sending a task force to 'nuke' their positions, we prefer to observe if allowed and then decide'. 'We will make a decision based on your report'. 'Good luck Eden 12 and we look forward to your detailed report in 30 days'....'Eden 12 stands up quickly, excited at going back to the mountains and thanks his commanding officers for the opportunity. Eden 12 quickly walks back to his pod checking a nuclear stick out along his way. Eden 12 gets into his pod and blasts out of the hole in the ground and heads vertically for the cloud cover not allowing his pod to get horizontal until he has broken through the cloud cover. Eden 12 sits back into his seat as the pod reaches its maximum speed and he smiles to himself, 'today is looking like it's going to be a great day', he says out loud. And he punches the EMD into life as it tracks him to the coordinates set by the commanders.

As his craft lurches to the left and then swings fast and dives towards the mountains he notices the peak he was connected to as the pod gently lands and sucks itself down onto the green lush vegetation almost disappearing into the soft wet undergrowth. Eden 12 shoots out of the pod and lands a few meters from a sleek rowing scull positioned by a prior scouting party. Eden 12 notes its simplicity of design and its sheer symmetry as he climbs on board and clamps his feet into the perfectly engineered foot slots. As he glides away he can see how the perfect symmetrical scull has a fine precision and balance and feels the optimum point to place the boat before adding some considerable force to the oars. Eden 12 glides silently and quickly through the clear cold waters hardly making a ripple as he reaches for a deep point in the water with the oars and with incredible strength sends the scull flying forward. As Eden 12 settles into an optimum pace he hears the shrill cries of the bird he witnessed on his last visit and he looks up as the giant bird circles the canyon and follows him as he winds his way through the narrow chasm in the rocks. The river opens up as he approaches the lake and he notices that he is being escorted by a large grey wolf that has spotted him and it is keeping pace with him along the river's edge. The wolf keeps one eye on him the other on its way through the undergrowth. As he emerges into the lake he spots the magnificent willow tree now full of white blossom looking resplendent as it languishes on the bank its fine petals floating and twisting towards the lake and gently landing in small circles adding to the beauty of the scene. Eden 12 tenses briefly as he spots a black object on one of the lower branches, he was alerted initially by two yellow piercing eyes in the shadows as a big black cat stares at the sight of Eden 12 gliding quickly past the tree and towards the opposite shore.

Standing passively to greet him all in white with his sword glinting in the sunlight is the warrior who had provided his escape. As Eden 12 glides up onto the sandy bank with one last pull of the oars, the warrior remains as stationary as ever, as Eden 12 unclamps his feet from the bindings and walks towards the warrior he bows and Eden 12 copies the act from one of the film clips he viewed, he adopts the same stance. Eden 12 unzips a pocket on his suit and unfolds the orange robe and pulls it over his head and again bows once more to the warrior. As Eden 12 takes his eyes away from the warrior for one slight moment, the warrior makes a move to Eden 12's right side and he is pushed down onto his knees, he remains there not daring to move a muscle or to engage further with any eye contact staring at the ground in front of him. Eden 12 remains in this position until the warrior glides silently and effortlessly up the sand to the steps and seems to float up the steps towards the summit. Eden 12 remains in the position until the next morning; throughout the night he sensed the big cat close to his position interested to see if he could be new prey but luckily it never attacked. The wolf howled all night and kept him from drifting into a deep sleep. Eden 12 started to shift his weight momentarily as the sun started to light up the lake and just as he was about to stand up an arrow grazed the top of his skull creating a deep ridge in its protective covering. Eden 12 quickly adopted his kneeling position before the next arrow kills him. Three days pass in this position and Eden 12 has to rely on his suit to recycle his body fluids to keep his body from closing down into a hypothermia stasis and as he gently and slowly lowers his head to check that the system is engaged a second arrow grazes his left arm ripping the suit like a hot knife through butter, the flap from his cut suit gently flaps in the breeze off the lake…Towards sunset the white warrior appears and drifts slowly down to his position and with the broad side of his sword smashes it into Eden 12's arm and shouts quickly and softly motioning him to rise. Eden 12 quickly got to his feet and again bowed to the warrior. The warrior circles him and with his elbow strikes Eden 12 with such force that he shoots forward and commences to walk a few paces as he does so another strike to his head keeps him from stopping and Eden 12 heads for the steps and he knows he has been accepted…With some trepidation and fear of upsetting his new master Eden12 negotiates the steps as quickly as he can with the warrior pushing him and keeping pace with him at every step.

Chapter 4

Eden 12 creeps silently along the ground of the cave and senses no human life forms, he tracks his way through the underground tunnels by the scratches he made in the wall as he entered. Using his night vision he can see clearly the deep grooves in the wall he made when he entered. He finally catches a glimpse of the entrance silhouetted by the moon as the rays of light form an arch over the floor. Eden 12 flies down the steps hardly touching them as his tough feet and limbs absorb the impact as he hurtles downwards. He feels the soft sand give way underneath him as he ploughs his feet into the sand and drives forward at an astonishing rate to the edge of the water; he stops suddenly and crouches down, scanning the horizon and pouring his gaze over the cliffs. He knows from experience that if he is being watched and they don't want him to leave then he is surely dead and if he manages to slip away and the monks are watching then they wanted it that way. The water of the lake laps at the canoes hull, still tethered to the post. He quickly unfastens the mooring and glides into the scull, easing the oars gently, silently and swiftly into the water, making no sound he powers his way across the lake. As he leaves the vast lake and approaches the entrance to the cliffs looming large on either side of him he senses something behind him and in the water tracking his movement? Eden 12 picks up his pace and wastes no time in reaching the reeds at the end of the river, he drives his scull into the reeds and launches himself out with a leap and plants himself in the weeds looking intently towards the river. Suddenly a craft breaks the surface of the water and thrusts itself to within feet of him landing softly in the reeds next to him.

The craft opens and he recognizes members of his platoon, he gets up and smiles greeting each member with a hug and a smile. 'Great to see you lot' Eden 12 says with a grin. 'We have been monitoring the area since you went in just in case you had any problems, Eden 15 shouts back. Eden 8 approaches Eden 12 and takes him by the arm and leads him to his pod, on the way he reminds Eden 12 of his mission and that he has to report back to HQ with his findings as soon as possible. 'We will be staying here to monitor the 'monks' so in the meantime take care and report in'. Eden 12 raises the pod door and climbs in, he turns on the EMD and he launches vertically at full power and quickly settles into cruising mode just on top of the clouds. Just as he settles back to enjoy the ride with the sun warming up his cockpit Eden 1 appears on his screen in front of him. Eden 12 welcome back I trust you are well, report to me and Eden 3 in the de-briefing room as soon as you dock please, thank you. 'Ok Sir, ETA about 20 clicks, see you shortly. Eden 12 once more sits back and contemplates his last 30 days with the monks and what he is going to say to his superiors? Eden 12 feels somewhat transformed by his time with the monks and has learned a lot in the last few days, he certainly wouldn't want to invoke any aggression towards them as they are ultimately a peaceful race and he feels that they can learn a great deal from them. The problem is with their incredibly fighting skills and defense mechanisms, given that they use them in any shape or form against his platoon, HQ will just 'Nuke' them out of existence. He needs to find a way to help preserve what he has found and somehow allow them to be left alone. However the policy with any race or mutant that lives on the surface for the last hundreds of years is to nuke it out of existence and that is what his platoon was primarily created for, to eradicate and eliminate any surface dwellers. Especially if they are perceived as a threat and the monks quite clearly are. The preferred option for dealing with any communities they find on the surface is simple EMP (Electro magnetic pulses) traveling at 106 miles per second are deployed that exploded in mid air and can cover a 300 miles radius with no blast recorded, they can localize the damage to a 30 miles radius if needed. The whole environment the monks live in would disappear in a matter of seconds proceeded by nuclear strikes that would level the mountain to the ground in minutes. Eden 12 was apprehensive as he dropped like a stone towards HQ and thundering back into the earth and docking gently in a parking bay. Eden 12 checked his weapon at the desk and walked briskly along the bright well lit corridor towards the briefing room. Eden 1 & 3 got out of their chairs and greeted him warmly, 'Sit down now and let us here what you have experienced over the last 30 days'. Well Sir I can report that the monks are no immediate threat to us and absolutely different from any life form we have encountered before'. I was well received and treated very kindly by the monks and introduced to their culture, they are not averse to sharing their skills and taught me certain aspects of their arts as well as introduced me to what is their religion, something connected with someone called 'Buddha'? The majority of the time is spent worshipping this 'Buddha' and their daily lives revolve around it, the rest of the time is spent on food production and exercise, this being in the form of fighting. But the general theme to their existence is peace and whilst I initially did encounter some threat it was only on the basis of defense and they would not have harmed me. No weapons exist of any kind other than primitive, wooden and steel weapons, and not technology in any form is evident, no vehicles of any type exist and they do not break the cloud cover and make their way towards the earth's surface. It seems they are an entirely forgotten race that points back to our early existence on the plant prior to its destruction and they have no desire to interact with any other aspect of the planet, they are entirely self supportive and pose no immediate threat to us. 'Thank you Eden 12 your report has been recorded and we will disseminate that to the council and all concerned with this discovery please report back to your cell until further notice. Eden 12 stood up and exited the room hoping that he didn't come across as to sympathetic to the monks, he hoped that the powers that be would for once see it not as a threat but something they can learn from, they are not mutants and intent on attacking our civilization they are peaceful people and Eden 12 wants to learn more if he can. Eden 12 docks into his home parking bay and steps out, inside his cell he takes of his suit, hangs it up and relaxes, in the pocket of his suit he pulls out a small little cone and matches and strikes the match on his rough skin, he burns the cone and puts it on his wash basin, he sits on the floor crossed legs closes his eyes and meditates as the monks had shown him.

Chapter 5

Eden 12 wakes and washes his face to wake himself. He grabs his torn robes and sits in a full lotus position on the floor in front of a little shrine he has made to Chenzrig the god of ultimate compassion. Eden 12 has been studying the monks past and has sourced a lot of information on a religion called Buddhism that he is using to follow on from what the monks have shown him whilst in their care. He picks up two sticks on his shrine and starts beating out a rhythmic on the beat pulse chanting at the same time. Kan-Ji-Zai, Bo-Sa, Gyo-Jin,Han-Nya-Ha-Ra-Mi-Ta Eden 12 chants for it seems forever as the words change he starts moving with the pulse of his sticks and staring down at his reading tablet follows the text to the end, finally he shouts, Han-Nya, Shin-Gyo….An intercom in his room blasts a command, Eden 12 report for briefing at 09.05hrs. This startles him and he quickly jumps to his feet reaching for his bio suit, as he closes his suit off, he grabs at some small capsules and swallows them pouring himself a glass of water to wash them down. Eden 12 jumps out of his capsule door and sprints down the hallway to the briefing room. When he arrives all the crew are already assembled and waiting, 'Sorry sir' Eden 12 gestures to Eden 2 who is standing on the plinth waiting for him to sit down. 'Men, further to our reconnaissance of the area at 234,567 other wise code named 'Cloud Mountain' we are to strike today and destroy the area completely. Eden 12 visibly shaken gasps and exclaims under his breath, 'no'. Eden 2 continues, 'you will proceed under my leadership to the rendezvous coordinates that have been assigned to your pods and you will wait for my commands. All pods have been loaded with multiple nuclear devices so I would suggest that close formation flying is avoided for obvious reasons and we should assume a delta pattern whilst navigating to the target. Eden 12, bellows, 'Is that clear?' 'Yes sir' the squad replies. 'Thank you' Eden 2 responds. 'Departure is at 09.30hrs. Eden 2 walks off the plinth and out of the briefing room and the squad start talking among themselves, some of them excited at using the nuclear devices for the first time. Somebody shouts to a group of new recruits, 'hey rookies make sure you point those things at the target and when you hit that button run like hell', all the experienced warriors erupt into laughter as the new Eden's file out looking rather sheepish and embarrassed by the old guard. Eden 15 approaches Eden 12 and slaps him on the back, 'what's up mate you gone over to the other side or something?' Eden 12 doesn't respond and pushes his hand off his shoulder with a shrug, Eden 12 head bowed walks out the room and sprints back to his capsule…Eden 12 in a state of panic cannot think of how to warn the monks on 'Cloud Mountain', what can he do he thinks over and over to himself, will the monks know they are about to be attacked? Eden 12 leaves his capsule and bumps into Eden 15 and some other older warriors, 'here he is our own resident monk himself' Eden 15 laughs. Eden 12 ignores them and sprints to his pod managing to open the door and slip in without any further interaction with his fellow crew. Eden 12 starts his craft and guns it down the access shoot to the surface, going ballistic as the pod enters the earth's atmosphere. Eden 12 shoots up towards the stars for a long time thinking of his mission wishing he could just keeping going upwards and straight into orbit. 'Eden 12' barks Eden 2, engage with the delta formation at 3 clicks North West of the colony. 'Dam' Eden 12 mutters and puts his pod into a reverse 720 degree roll and shoots off to the rest of his squadron at twice the speed of sound, achieving a massive crescendo as he smashes through the sound barrier. 'Sorry sir' Eden 12 reports back, ' I thought I spotted an alien craft so went vertical after the target'. 'Okay Eden 12, rejoin the squadron and take up the rear position'. Eden 12 slots into the formation and thinks to himself if he had enough warheads could he take out his squad, he ponders this as they race across the upper atmosphere of the plant. Below the black and grey planet interspersed with even blacker water reflects Eden 12's mood. Clouds on the horizon start to appear and Eden 2 shots to the squad, 'Okay men follow me and go to radar tracking set your distances to 20 metons to avoid collision in the clouds'. Each squad member disappears into the clouds and they are all separated from each other. Eden 12 monitors his radar and tracks each of his neighbor's crafts; he gets an alert and changes his position, toying with the idea of a suicidal act to wipe out the whole squad. The sky suddenly clears and 'Cloud Mountain' comes into view, the sun is shining and a flock of white birds drift effortlessly over the mountain top, he sees the temple at the summit of the mountain and the white stone reflects the sun back at them as they head for the rendezvous point just north of the mountain. Eden 12 cannot get over the brightness of the scenery and the way that the lake below reflects the splendor of the mountain in its slowly undulating waters. He still can't believe that they are all here for the sole purpose of wiping out this ancient civilization. Eden 2 calmly commands, 'Men I want you to form a line to the north west of the mountain at 5 metons apart'. The pods arrange themselves into a very distinct line, as Eden 12 lines his pod up he notices the area he first landed on when he discovered the mountain. Eden 2 now much calmer than ever before more or less whispers the next command as leaving all the squad to strain and focus on his words, 'Men this is very important, on my command release, multiple rockets at the designated target. Wait for at least no more than 2 seconds from release, and then leave the area in a 360 reverse flip. When horizontal punch the pod to mach 2 immediately and head in that level direction north until such time as I give you the order to stop'. At this point Eden 2, shouts, 'is that clear'? A loud, 'Yes sir' is the response. On my command release the warheads, 3-2-1, release. As Eden 12 flick the switches to release the warhead he counts to two as he watches multiple rockets race towards the mountain leaving huge plumes of white smoke in their wakes. He performs the 360 flip and punches the dash as his pod throws him back into his seat and reaches mach 2, banging through the sound barrier as it flies along. He keeps an eye on his rear view camera as he sees the rockets hit the target and multiple mushroom clouds rise up into the air leaving nothing but a black dense smoke behind…He then sees multiple objects chasing them away from the area the devastated vegetation and other obstacles all blown out from the impact of the explosion race away from the mountain with them…Eden 2, trying to calm his voice, shouts a command, 'Well done men, this is critical on my mark we have to descend back through the clouds at the same time, again set your radar to track at 20 metons apart. On my mark descend 10000 metons, 3-2-1, mark. Tracking each other the squad descends, however as they dive into the clouds turbulence from the explosion hits then and the pods start being blown around like rain drops. Eden 12 cannot control his craft and let's go as its tracker tries desperately to avoid any other pod and keep the distance between then all. Blind to the presence of any of his squad he sits tight and grasps his seat with both hands. As he starts to gain visibility a pod is blown straight up into his path and they collide, both pods spin wildly away from each other breaking formation.

Eden 12 is heading down towards the earth's surface as his fellow squad member like a skittle ball collides with the rest of his squad in formation and three of the pods instantly explode. Eden 12 in a rotating spin sees the debris of flames pour down after him as he tries to gain control of his craft. The pod is going too fast to level out and its spinning motion is so intense that Eden 12 is starting to lose consciousness. He quickly grabs at a lever near his seat and he is fired like a rocket out of the pod, a bubble closes around him and rockets fire downwards to stop his rate of descent, bringing him to a halt just from the surface of the air. The bubble is designed to hover until rescue and its beacons and communications have been deployed. 'Eden 12, come in Eden 12', shouts a voice through his communications. 'Affirmative Eden 12 here'. 'Eden 12, this is Eden 3, we have lost squad leader Eden 2 in the collision and I will send a rescue crew to you in due course, remain in your bubble until discovery, is that clear Eden 12. 'Affirmative sir'. Eden 12 sits back and scans the horizon for any hostile entities, luckily he has landed in a swamp region and not many predators can survive out here so far from the main land as the swamp consists of a chemical nightmare to most creatures. ….Sat suspended in his escape 'bubble' Eden 12 contemplates his last mission, he knew deep down that it was a bad idea to attack and destroy the monks hideout and he feels partly responsible for its demise. With one eye on the horizon scanning for his rescue craft and the other on his on board systems he tries to dial up any visuals of the last mission but his screens just omit this green glare with nothing becoming visible. He is aware that his escape 'bubble' can only resist gravity for a limited number of hours and he really needs to leave the craft before it starts to sink into the poisonous swamps a feet below him. He looks into the swamp and can see some writing and red lights that appear to him like some kind of old transportation vehicle from many centuries ago. It is lightly covered over with water and he can still see what looks like a child's toy floating behind its rear windows looking back at him with its dead but joyful eyes staring back at him. His eyes are suddenly diverted quickly to a glowing white orb like shape in the distance travelling very quickly towards him. He was not familiar with the craft and it was moving so fast his instincts prepare him to defend his position. He triggers the defenses on the escape craft but nothing responds. He arms his hand held weapon and he can only wait until impact knowing that if it is a missile he cannot survive. As the glow gets to within a few feet of him and as he braces himself for impact it stops dead in its tracks.

The glow suddenly manifests itself as a person, translucent and white with a light that pervades every aspect of his surroundings. In a split second Eden 12 is back at the Monks hideaway and his craft is gently resting on the beach close the lakes edge. He quickly opens the craft and prepares for his escape, heading deftly for the water's edge he notices the silhouette of a bright object hovering above him in the water he looks up and the entity fixes his stare upon him and in the next split second they are transported deep into the mountain. Eden 12 activates his night vision but doesn't need it for long as the brightly glowing being approaches him and fixes his gaze as he does so he hears someone talking to him as though communicating with him in the same room. Eden 12 spins around and checks the area in a 360 degree spin but cannot see anyone with them. The voice shouts 'stop' and Eden freezes to the spot. The voice is being transmitted by telepathy from the white glowing being in front of him and at that point it smiles. Close up he notices the beauty of the being and it is female and as the glow recedes he can make out its appearance. The female creature looks very young with jet black hair piled high on her head with what look like jewels in her hair. Fine green necklaces adorn her neck and in one hand she is holding a flower and in her hand a tiny dagger with a tip like a diamond and a handle that ends with a gold sphere that seems to glow and have some kind of energy attached to it. In the dark and at her feet he notices animal scales of some kind and the creature's feet are huge claws and he keeps getting a glimpse every time her white dress moves and dances around her body. As the light continues to recede from the her body he has to rely more on his night vision and can only now see an outline of the girl that appears to have a moon like object behind her head and he notices a huge bow that seems to tie the girls dress in half. The girl points her dagger towards the caves wall and it splits and a gaping hole appears she ushers him forward with her talons and he stand near the gap in the wall looking down into a huge space. A stream of what looks like people seems to be flowing high into the air then as it reaches infinity it seems to rush down and around again with a screaming noise unlike anything he has heard before. He looks across at the girl for guidance and she smiles. 'Migrating souls', he hears her say to him. 'Thousands of migrating souls', he repeats to himself. Suddenly people appear in front of them as they break off from the stream and flow of the movement and they approach them in the cave walking through the walls and walking through the girl they seem be trying to enter her body but as they do so and are repelled they scream and cry out returning back to the huge space in front of them. Over in the distance huge creatures are taunting those who are wandering around the space still searching for a way out and as they try to make contact with the huge creatures they are ripped apart and their body parts are thrown everywhere with, limbs and heads being savaged and eaten. 'The meat of human heads' she states and as he looks at the girl she has a round silver tray in her hands with five human heads lying in a circle on it. Eden 12 jumps back in horror as she throws the human heads into the gap in the wall and they disappear into the void. The girl laughs and smiles and says to him, 'Let's go'. They arrive in the temple he remembers from his last visit and nothing is changed

, they didn't destroy the target after all, but how could that be he thinks to himself they used enough nuclear fusion to destroy the planet? The girl talks to him again, 'Eden 12 this is what we call 'Dream Mountain' it is our space a collective space that we have created over many centuries and lifetimes'. 'You have been lucky enough due to experience this phenomena for reasons unknown to yourself but it is for you a true experience and fact that you can interact here and in our collective space'. 'Only we know why you are here and all will be revealed to you in time'. 'Whilst this construct appears solid to you and your species thought they could destroy it no physical intervention can do any harm to this place and it is like attacking a dream or mirage and none of your weapons or species can destroy what is created here'. 'The aftermath of your attack is purely the result of attacking what was not there in the first place and the consequences have been experienced by you and the rest of your species'. 'Some of you survived and some of you died in the attack, but what is clear is that you are connected to us and for now that is all that matters'. 'Your craft is as it was over on the other side of the lake and you are free to make your choices yet again'. 'You are free to go or you are free to stay and learn more about us?'. Eden 12 could see his pod on the other side of the lake and sheltered by the huge trees branches. He fell to his knees and put his head into his hands.

Printed in Great Britain
by Amazon